DUE DATE

		APR 4	1992
MAR 5 1987		SEP 8	1992
APR 2 3 1987		AUG 3 1	
MAY 1 8 1987		AUG 2 9 1995	
		NOV 1 6 1999	
SEP 1 2 1987			
		DISCARDED	
OCT 1 1987			
DEC 7 1987		28 1987	
		JUN 2 5 1998	
APR 2 8 1988			
MAY 2 0 1988		31	
SEP 1 9 1991		Printed in USA	

For Iuop Cvtlep
D.L.

With love to my grandchildren
F.W.

The Sneeze
Text copyright © 1986 by David Lloyd
Illustrations copyright © 1986 by Fritz Wegner
First published in England by Walker Books Ltd, London.
Printed in Italy. All rights reserved.
Library of Congress Catalog Card Number: 85–46022
ISBN 0-694-00135-X
ISBN 0-397-32196-1 (lib. bdg.)
First American Edition

THE
SNEEZE

by David Lloyd

pictures by Fritz Wegner

J. B. LIPPINCOTT   NEW YORK

Once upon a time there were

a hat

a bench

a ball

a girl

a dog

a man

a newspaper

a suitcase

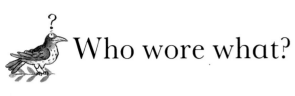 # Who wore what?

Did the man wear the hat?

Did the girl wear the newspaper?

Did the dog wear the suitcase?

The girl wore the hat.

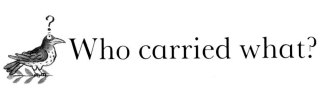 Who carried what?

Did the man carry the dog?

Did the dog carry the suitcase?

Did the girl carry the bench?

The man carried the suitcase.

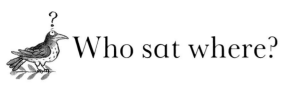 # Who sat where?

Did the dog sit on the bench?

Did the girl sit on the hat?

Did the man sit on the ball?

The man sat on the bench.

 # Who read what?

Did the dog read the newspaper?

Did the girl read the suitcase?

Did the man read the dog?

The man read the newspaper.

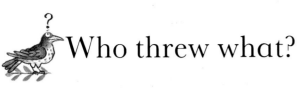 # Who threw what?

Did the man throw the bench?

Did the girl throw the man?

Did the dog throw the ball?

The girl threw the ball.

Did the man jump over the dog?

Did the girl jump over the suitcase?

Did the dog jump over the girl?

The dog jumped over the suitcase.

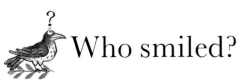 # Who smiled?

Did the man smile?

Did the dog smile?

Did the girl smile?

The girl smiled.

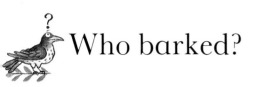 # Who barked?

Did the man bark?

Did the dog bark?

Did the girl bark?

The dog barked.

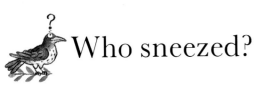 Who sneezed?

Did the man sneeze?

Did the dog sneeze?

Did the girl sneeze?

The man sneezed.

So what was the story?

The man carrying the suitcase

sat down on the bench and

started reading the newspaper.

The girl in the hat walked by with the dog.

The girl threw the ball.

The dog jumped over the suitcase.

The girl smiled.

The dog barked.

The man sneezed.

And what was in the suitcase?

The largest handkerchief in the whole wide world.